Merry Modern Christmas!

Vincent Spada
Illustrated by Blake Schneider

Amazing Things Press

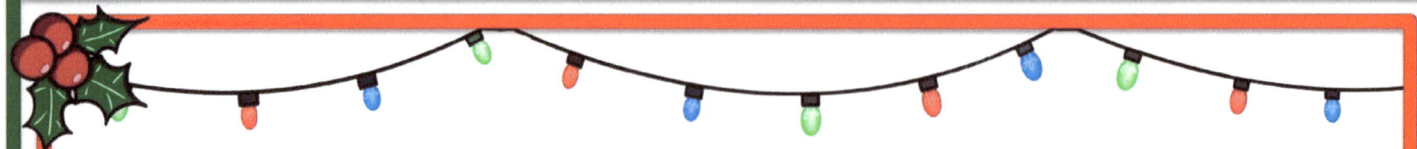

Illustrations by Blake Schneider
Book design by Julie L. Casey

ISBN 979-8887260549
Printed in the United States of America.

For more information, visit
www.amazingthingspress.com

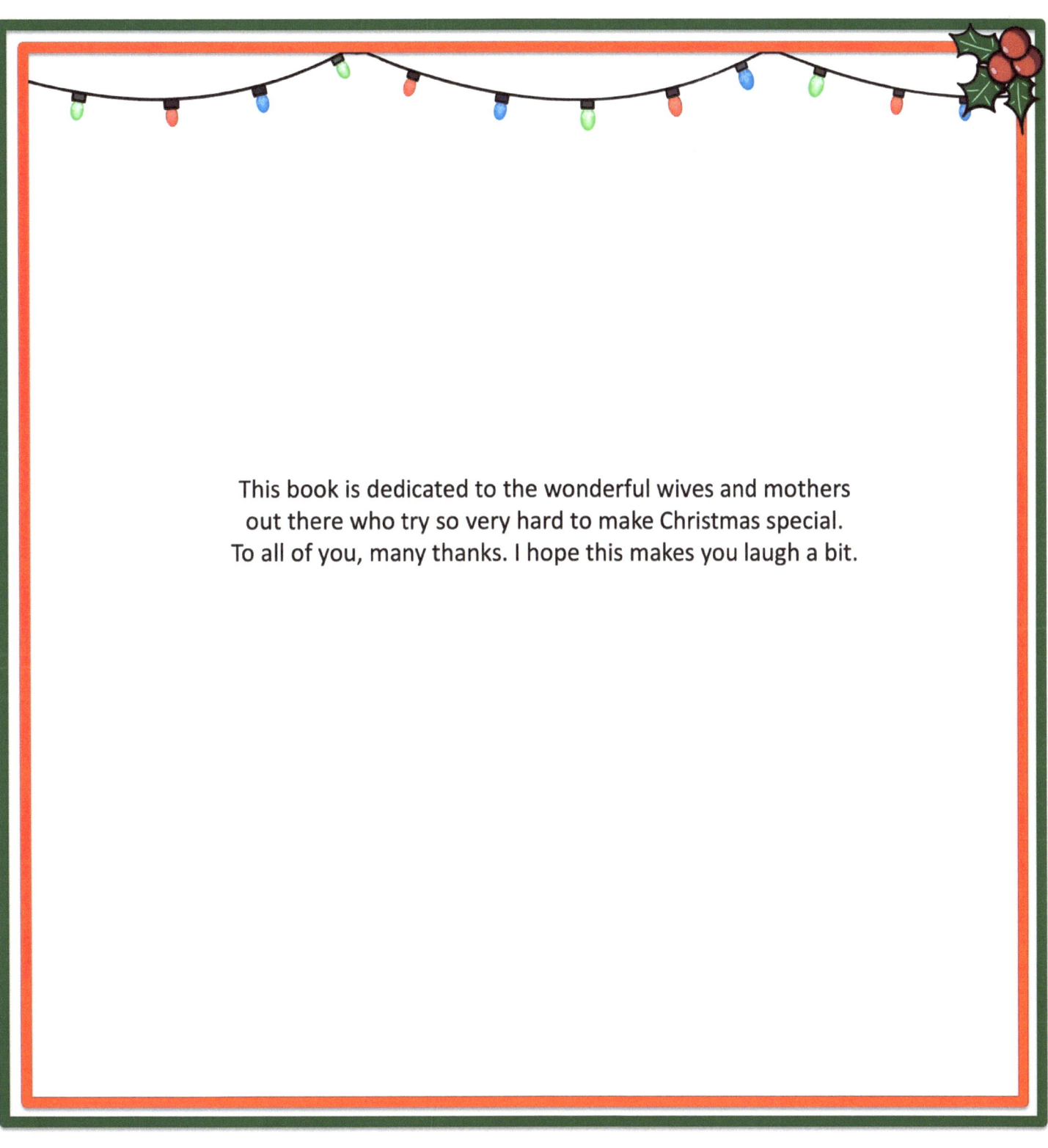

This book is dedicated to the wonderful wives and mothers
out there who try so very hard to make Christmas special.
To all of you, many thanks. I hope this makes you laugh a bit.

'Twas the day before Christmas, and things were a mess.
All the kids were a' screaming and building my stress.

The cookies were smoking, all burned with the bread,
while visions of firemen danced in my head.

The dog kept on howling and pawing the door,
and then took a whiz all over my floor.

When I went to mop it, to my great surprise,
he then took a crap right in front of my eyes!

But in walked my daughter, a freshman in college, and gave me an earful of her endless "knowledge"!

Before I could slap her, she walked off all haughty,
and in came my son with a grin rather naughty.

When I questioned his look, he shrugged like he's simple, then squeezed his face, and zit-popped a big pimple!

Now sick from this sight, I returned to my baking.
My feet were all swollen, my back all a' aching.

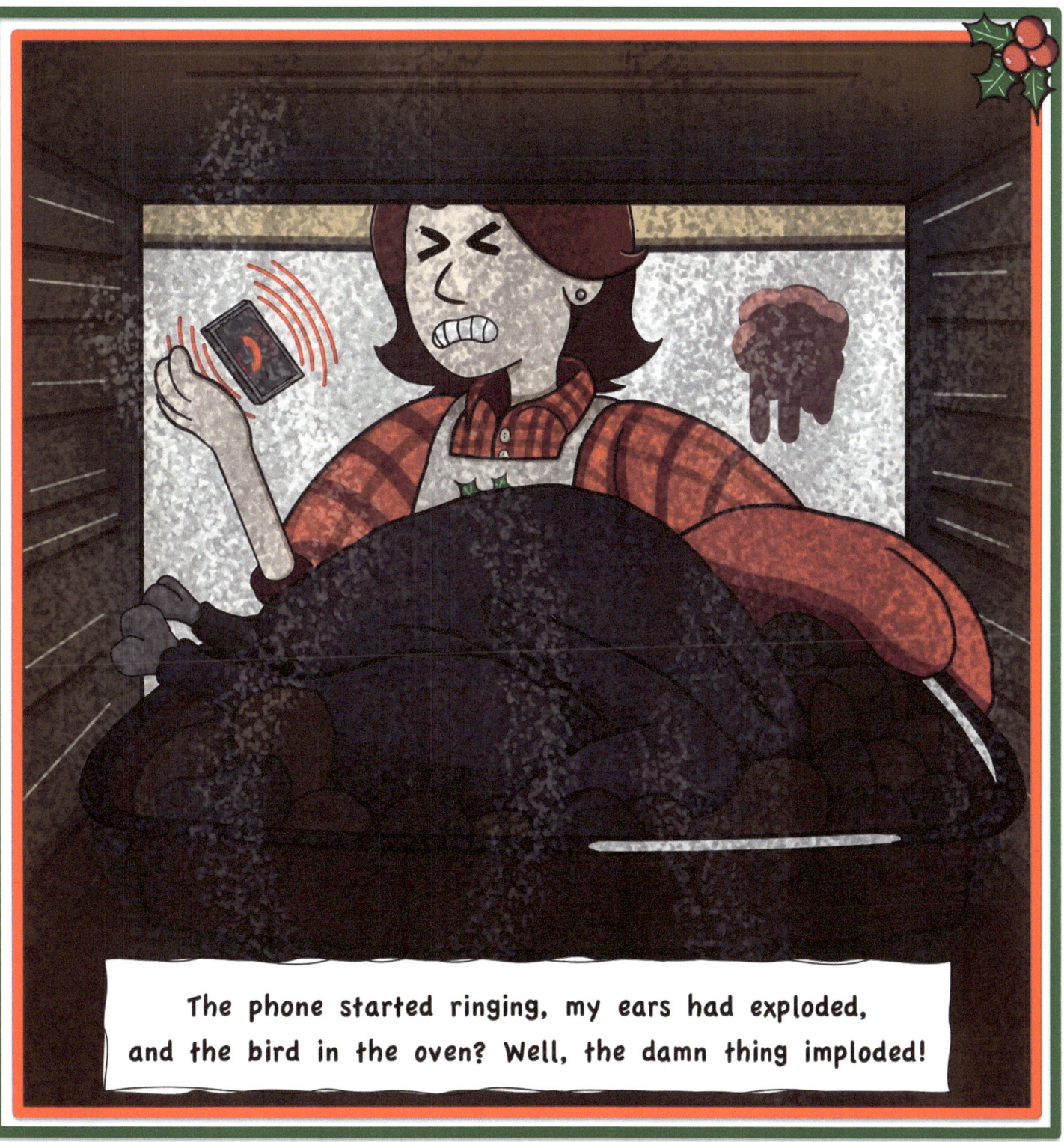

The phone started ringing, my ears had exploded,
and the bird in the oven? Well, the damn thing imploded!

My arms baked and crispy, I sank down to my knees.
I wanted to quit and just order Chinese!

But no! I was hosting and must wear a brave smile.
So I went on a' cooking, this practice so vile.

At last! After hours full of tears, sweat, and burns,
I set the table myself; no one else friggin' learns.

The guests had arrived, and their moods were so cheery.
Especially drunk Aunt Matilda, who just kept saying "dearie"!

He'd brought his pet lizard for some silly reason,
but I guess reptiles are perfect for the holiday season!

So there on my lap sat my youngest with glee,
flinging cranberry sauce all over—you guessed it—ME!

My grandma was laughing until her dentures spat out, and my dad, after farting, complained of his gout.

My grandpa, for fun, started with the dirty joking.
He chuckled and snorted and soon he was choking!

My husband, the jackass, had finally awoke,
and my father-in-law, the chimney, continued to smoke.

So there in the darkness, among the great din,
I poured a tall glass of eggnog, sat back, and gave in.

And you'll understand, if you've known this same plight.
So screw Merry Christmas and have a good night!

Merry
Christmas
to all!

About the Illustrator

Blake Schneider has illustrated several books, including *Elmo Engine Saves the Day* and *Travis Tractor Goes to the Fair* by T.R. Henson, and *Merry Modern Christmas* by Vincent Spada (Amazing Things Press 2024).

About the Author

Vincent Spada is a poet and children's author for such titles as *The Ultimate Baseball Trivia Book* (Quarto Publishing, 2025), *When the World Runs Out of Snow* (Penbard, 2024), *Mercy Methuen*, and *Joe Racoon*. He also pens screenplays and short-story collections from his native New England.

A Message from the Author

Thank you for taking the time to read my book.
I would be honored if you would
consider leaving a review for it on ***Amazon***.

Check out all our children's books at
www.amazingthingspress.com/childrens-picture-books.html
or visit our website by scanning the QR code below.